# The
# Book
# With
# No
# Pictures

## B.J. Novak

Dial Books for Young Readers
an imprint of Penguin Group (USA) LLC

This is a book with
no pictures.

It might seem like no fun to have someone read you a book with no pictures.

It probably seems
*boring*
and
*serious.*

Except...

Here is how books work:

Everything the words say, the person reading the book *has to say.*

No matter what.

That's the deal.

That's the rule.


So that means...

Even if the words say...

# BLORK.

Wait—what?

That doesn't even
mean anything.

# BLuuRF.

Wait a second—what?!

This isn't the kind
of book I wanted to
read!

And I have to say
every word the book says?

Uh-oh...

# I am a monkey who taught myself to read.

Hey! I'm not
a monkey!

And now I am reading you this book with my **monkey mouth** in my **monkey voice.**

That's not true...
I am not a monkey!

Yes, I am

**a monkey.**

# Also, I am a

# ROBOT

# MONKEY.

WHAT?!

And my head
is made of
**blueberry
pizza.**

Wait a second—

Is this whole book
# a trick?

Can I stop reading,
please?

## No?!!

And now it's time for me to sing you my favorite song!

A song?

Do I really have to sing a—

♫ glug
glug
glug ♫
my face is a
bug... ♫
♫
♫

I eat ants for ♫

**breakfast**

right off the

ruuuuuuug!

What?!

This book is ridiculous!

Can I stop reading yet?

No?!?

There are MORE pages?!

I have to read the rest?!?!

My only friend in the whole wide world is a hippo named

BOO
BOO
BUTT

BooBooButt?!

and also,
the kid I'm reading
this book to is

THE BEST

IN THE HISTORY OF

# KID EVER

## THE ENTIRE WORLD

Oh, really?

and this kid is the
smartest kid
too, because this kid
chose this book
even though it had
no pictures

because kids know
this is the book
that makes grown-ups
have to say
**silly things!**

and...

make silly sounds like...

oh no oh no here it comes...

# GLuURR-
## GA-WOCKO
# ma
# GRUMPH-
### a-doo
# AiiEE! AiiEE!
# AiiEE!!!
# BRROOOOoOG
# BRROOoOOG
# BRROOOOoOG

# OOOOOOOmph!

# EEEEEEEmph!

**Blaggity-BLaGGITY**

GLIBBITY-globbity

globbity-GLIBBITY

BEEP. BOOP.

eeeeeeeeeeeeeeeeeeeeeeeeeeeeeeee
eeeeeeeeeeeeeeeeeeeeeeeeeeeeeeee
eeeeeeeeeeeeeeeeeeeeeeeeeeeeeeee
eeeeeeeeeeeeeeeeeeeeeeeeeeeeeeee
eeeeeeeeeeeeeeeeeeeeeeeeeeeeeeee

# Ba-DOOONGY FACE!!!!!

Oh

my

goodness.

Please don't
**ever**
make me read
this book again!

It is so... **silly!**

In fact, it is completely
and utterly

**preposterous!**

Next time,

please please please please

**please**

choose a book with pictures.

Please?

Because this is just too

**ridiculous**

to read.

# The End

**BONK.**

I didn't want to say that.

*To the reader*
*and the future reader*

DIAL BOOKS FOR YOUNG READERS
Published by the Penguin Group
Penguin Group (USA) LLC
375 Hudson Street
New York, New York 10014

USA / Canada / UK / Ireland / Australia / New Zealand / India / South Africa / China
penguin.com
A Penguin Random House Company

CIP available upon request

Manufactured in the United States of America
10 9 8 7

Text set in Sentinel, Gotham and Visitor BRK Ten Pro